The carousel music grew louder and the horses swooped through the air as they gathered speed. The breeze blew on Laura's cheeks, and the fairground lights seemed to glitter and twinkle around her. To her surprise the breeze felt warm, like on a summer's day, and the air began to glow and shimmer like a summery mist. She looked up and gasped.

It was no longer a cool autumn evening – instead the sky was a beautiful bright blue, with the sun blazing down. And she wasn't holding on to the golden pole any more. She had real leather reins in one hand and a rope lasso in the other!

Also available

Sparkle

Brightheart

Jewel

Look out for

Crystal

Flame

MACMILLAN CHILDREN'S BOOKS

A Working Partners Book

With special thanks to Gill Harvey

First published 2006 by Macmillan Children's Books
a division of Macmillan Publishers Limited
20 New Wharf Road, London N1 9RR
Basingstoke and Oxford
www.panmacmillan.com

Associated companies throughout the world

ISBN-13: 978-0-330-44043-1
ISBN-10: 0-330-44043-8

Created by Working Partners Limited

1 3 5 7 9 8 6 4 2

A CIP catalogue record for this book is available from the British Library.

Printed and bound in Great Britain by Mackays of Chatham plc, Kent

Contents

1. A Starry Trip to the Fair

"Look! It's a lasso stall!" cried Laura. "Let's try that next!" She ran across the fairground, with her three brothers chasing after her. They all loved anything to do with the Wild West!

As they waited in the queue to throw lassos over different prizes, Laura hopped from foot to foot. "Come *on*, come *on*," she chanted.

Suddenly she heard a voice booming across the fairground. "Roll up, roll up for the most exciting ride of your lives!

Choose your favourite pony and let Barker's Magic Pony Carousel whisk you away on an amazing adventure! Ride a circus pony, a princess's pony, or a cowgirl's pony straight from the Wild West . . ."

"Did you hear that?" Laura gasped. She loved riding ponies as much as she loved the Wild West – a cowgirl's pony sounded the most exciting thing in the whole world! She looked hopefully at her oldest brother, Sam. "Can I have a ride on the Magic Carousel, please?"

"You and your ponies." Sam grinned. "OK. But I don't think the carousel's a ride for me. I'll just watch."

"Thanks!" said Laura.

They left Laura's other brothers, Harry and Paul, in the queue for the lasso stall and

made their way to Mr Barker's Magic Carousel.

Close up, the carousel's twinkling lights glowed merrily in the early evening light. Laura stared at the swirling red, gold and silver colours, desperate for a glimpse of the cowgirl's pony. There was the circus pony with a sparkly feather headdress, and a majestic medieval princess's pony with a

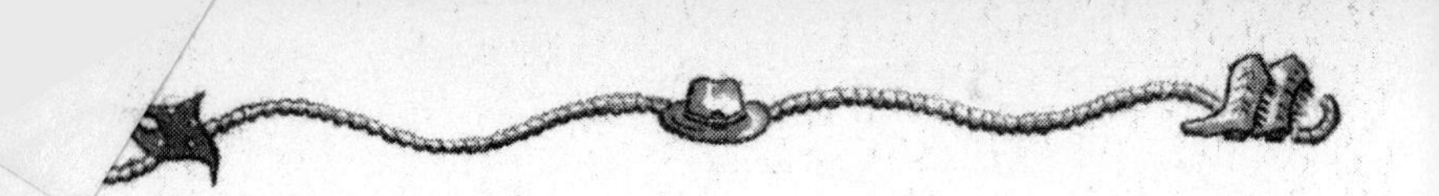

proudly arched neck . . . but where was the cowgirl's pony?

Then Laura saw her, the most beautiful pony on the carousel! She was a rich golden chestnut colour all over, apart from a star on her forehead. She wore a fancy leather bridle and a heavy tan-coloured Western saddle. Lara thought she looked just like the ponies in her favourite movies!

"Roll up, roll up!" called a tall man in a red and green stripy top hat. "Choose your favourite pony!" He caught sight of Laura. "Hello, young lady! I'm Mr Barker. Welcome to my magnificent Magic Carousel!"

Laura smiled. Mr Barker had such friendly, twinkling eyes! "I think I know which pony I want," she said.

"Well, that's a good start. But has that

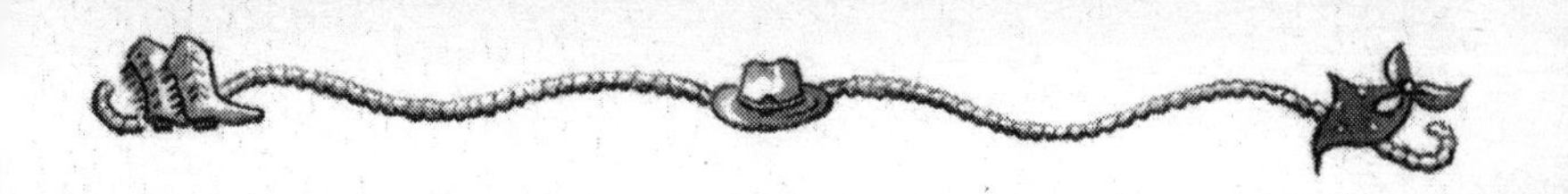

pony been chosen for you?" asked Mr Barker mysteriously.

Laura was puzzled. "What do you mean?" she asked.

Mr Barker laughed and lifted his stripy top hat. There was a flash of pink paper as he pulled something out from under it. It was a ticket! Laura glanced at Sam to see if he'd seen how the ticket had appeared, but he was busy looking at the ponies on the carousel.

"This is yours," said Mr Barker, handing her the ticket.

Laura looked at the ticket. There was a name written on it in swirling gold writing.

"Star!" she read out breathlessly. The cowgirl's pony had a star on her forehead – could that be her name? Feeling excited, she ran over to the carousel to take a closer look. The horse's name was written on her name-scroll.

"It says Star here too!" she said.

"Then that's the pony for you," said Mr Barker.

Star's painted brown eyes seemed to be encouraging her, so Laura clambered quickly on to the carousel. The Western saddle was very different from the English saddles she was used to. It was much more complicated, with a big horn at the front, lots of ropes and leather pouches, and stirrups that were much longer. But as the carousel began to turn, she felt so safe and comfortable that it was as if she'd always

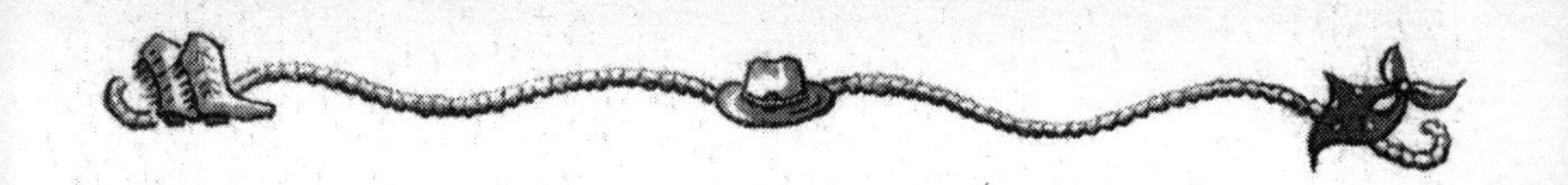

known how to ride a cowgirl's pony.

Laura waved at Sam, who grinned and waved back. The carousel music grew louder, and the horses swooped through the air as they gathered speed. The breeze blew on Laura's cheeks, and the fairground lights seemed to glitter and twinkle around her. To her surprise the breeze felt warm, like on a summer's day, and the air began to glow and shimmer like a summery mist. She looked up and gasped.

It was no longer a cool autumn evening – instead the sky was a beautiful bright blue, with the sun blazing down. And she wasn't holding on to the golden pole any more. She had real leather reins in one hand and a rope lasso in the other!

Laura blinked. When she opened her eyes again, she could see Star's chestnut mane

flying in the breeze. Dust swirled around her, and the sound of thundering hoofs filled her ears. Her jacket had disappeared – instead, she was wearing a pink and white checked shirt with the sleeves rolled up, a spotted kerchief around her neck, denim jeans and beautiful pale leather cowboy boots. The fairground had gone and she was cantering alongside a long line of cattle

that stretched far ahead, across a rolling plain. The cattle were all colours – brown and white, speckled and patchy – and they all had big, dangerous-looking horns.

Laura shielded her eyes against the sun. She could see a river up ahead, and in the distance rocky mountains jutted into the sky. There were other riders cantering beside the cattle too, wearing wide-brimmed hats and long leather chaps.

"Wow!" Laura exclaimed. "It's a Wild West cattle drive!"

2. Danger Ahead!

Laura didn't have time to wonder how she'd got there. Some of the cattle were bellowing loudly and she wanted to keep a close eye on those pointy horns! She concentrated on holding her reins – it was tricky having them in just one hand, but she remembered from watching Western movies that she had to rest the reins against the pony's neck to tell her which way to go.

Just as she was getting the hang of it, she heard a shout from behind her. Alarmed, she looked round. There was a

girl galloping towards her on a brown and white pony, and she looked very cross! She was wearing a buttercup-yellow shirt, and her glossy black pigtails were tied with yellow ribbons.

Laura opened her mouth to speak, but she didn't get a chance.

"Rope that steer!" cried the girl, pointing past Laura. "What are you waiting for?"

Laura twisted round and saw a young calf bolting away from the rest of the herd.

Its spindly legs were a blur as it raced off in a panic – straight towards the river!

Gripping her lasso tighter, Laura wheeled Star after the calf and kicked her into a gallop. She looked down at the rope in her right hand. Laura had seen cowboys in films lasso stampeding cattle, but she felt very nervous about attempting it herself.

"Swing . . . it around . . . a few times . . ." said a breathless voice. "Before you throw it!"

Laura glanced around, but there was no one there. Just herself and Star, galloping after the calf.

"It's me . . . Star!" puffed the voice as the pony's hoofs thundered across the dry, hard ground. "We've come here by magic . . . from the carousel. We have something very important to do . . . before I take you back!"

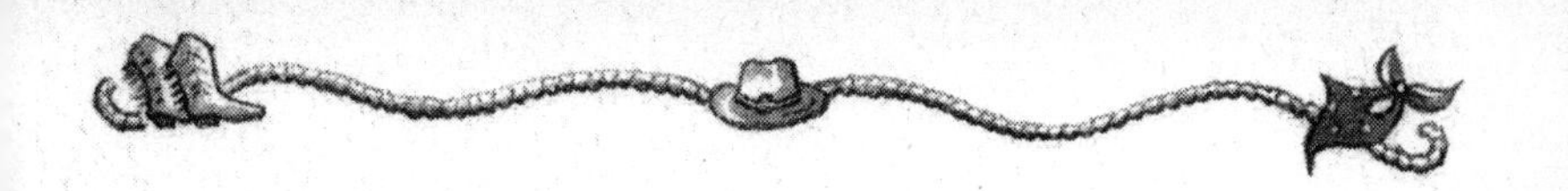

Laura nearly fell out of the saddle in surprise. "Star!" she gasped. "You can talk!"

"Hurry up!" shouted the girl with pigtails. Laura looked over her shoulder and saw that the brown and white pony was catching them up.

The calf was getting closer and closer to the river. Laura knew she didn't have time to ask Star any questions about the carousel. Somehow she had to get the hang of using her lasso. She leaned sideways out of the saddle and stretched her hand towards the calf.

"Quick, or you'll lose him!" called the girl.

"Ignore her," panted Star. "Just concentrate on the rope . . . It's all about . . . timing. I'll try not to . . . frighten the calf."

Laura's heart was pounding wildly. The

calf looked so small and helpless, and she could hear it calling out in fear. It was only a few paces from the river now, which looked big and wide with swirling currents of fast-flowing, muddy water. Laura noticed a branch being swept along until it smashed against a boulder. The calf wouldn't stand a chance if it fell in!

"Please stop, little calf," Laura pleaded. "Please!"

But the calf kept on running. Then, just as it was about to plunge into the river, it skidded to a halt on the muddy bank.

Star stopped at once. "I don't want to startle it," she whispered to Laura. "You should be able to rope it from here."

Laura glanced behind her. The brown and white pony had stopped too, but he was stamping restlessly, tugging at the bit.

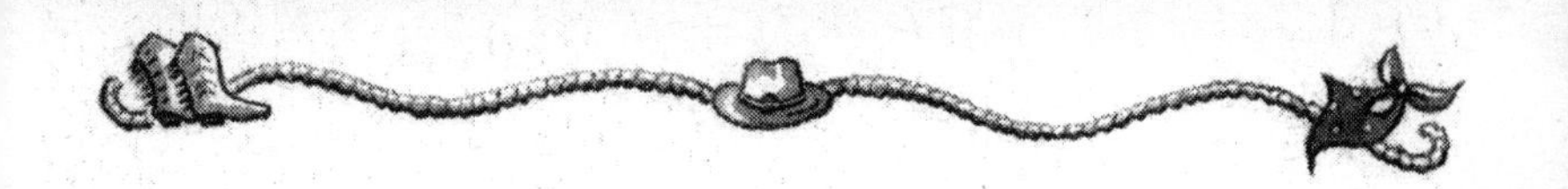

"I can't come any closer!" called the girl. "If I do, I'll frighten the calf even more. You'll have to rope him yourself!"

Laura nodded. The calf stood with his tiny hoofs sinking into the mud at the edge of the river. His big brown eyes were wide with fear.

"Stay there," Laura murmured, lifting the lasso. "Just stay right there!"

She lifted the lasso and began to swing it around above her head, feeling the coil of rope spin faster and faster through the air. But just as she was about to throw it the other girl's pony kicked a stone and sent it clattering towards the river. With a bleat of panic, the calf plunged straight into the swirling water!

Laura kicked Star forward at once. The calf was already being swept downstream, his

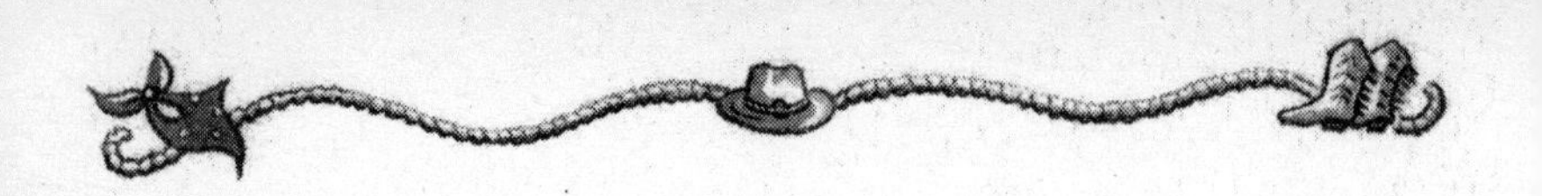

head only just above the surface. With a brave whinny, Star splashed into the river and Laura flung the lasso as hard as she could.

"I've got him!" she cried as the rope slipped over the calf's neck and shoulders.

"Now wind the rope around the saddle horn," instructed Star. "I'll try to dig my hoofs into the mud while you pull him in."

Beneath her, Laura could feel the pony struggling to keep her balance. The current was almost too strong for a sturdy cowgirl's pony, never mind a calf! Laura heaved on the rope, winding it around the strong piece of leather at the front of Star's saddle. The wet rope dug into her fingers, but she kept on pulling.

Suddenly Star slipped, and Laura lurched forward.

"Oh no!" she gasped as the rope dragged

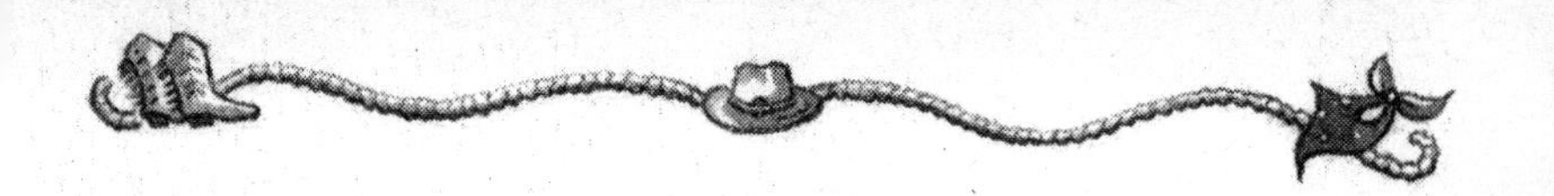

through her fingers and the calf bobbed further away.

"It's OK," muttered Star through gritted teeth. "I've got my footing now. Don't give up!"

Laura hauled on the rope again. It felt as though her arms were going to drop off, and the calf didn't seem any nearer! She could hear shouts from behind her, but they were muffled by the roar of the river. Inch by inch, Star slowly stepped back towards the bank. At last she was wading out of the water on to dry land. Laura gave a few final tugs on the rope and the calf stumbled out of the river on trembling legs.

Laura flung her arms around Star's neck. The pony was still out of breath and her nostrils were flaring, but her eyes were friendly and calm.

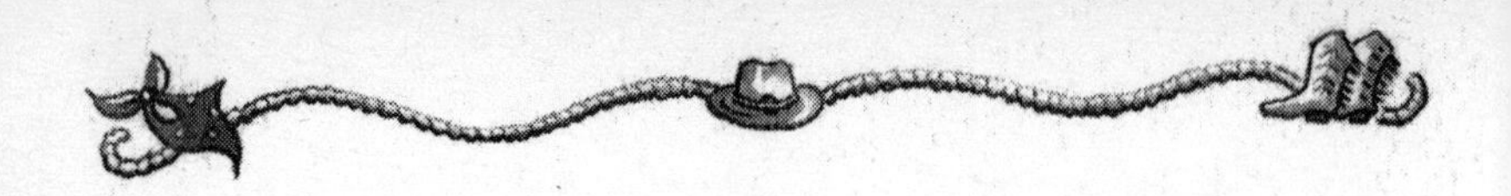

"Thank you so much!" Laura whispered. Then she slid out of Star's saddle to stroke the calf. He gave a grateful lick to the back of Laura's hand. His coat was soaked and muddy but she didn't care. He was safe, thanks to Laura and Star, and that was all that mattered!

3. Laura Earns Her Spurs

"Well done!" cried a voice, and Laura looked up. A cowboy was walking towards her, wearing a big grey hat and dusty, well-worn jeans. He was leading his horse, which was a strong-looking bay with a stripe down his face. "We saw what happened," he said. "You were really brave to go into the river!"

Laura hugged the small calf one last time. He had stopped shivering and his big brown eyes no longer looked afraid. She stood up and placed her hand on Star's

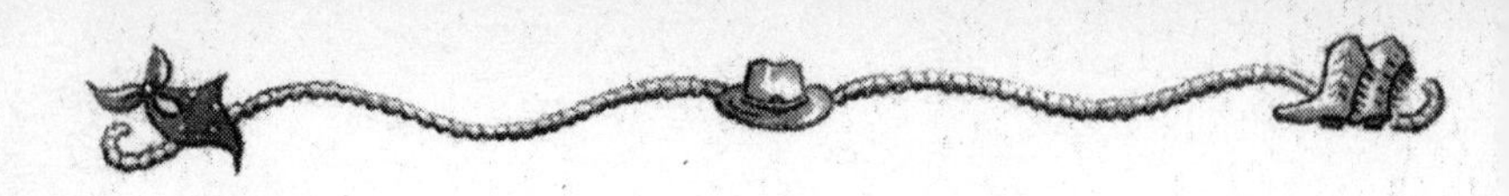

warm chestnut neck. Six or seven other men followed the cowboy in the grey hat. They looked like characters from the Western movies that Laura watched with her brothers, with their tanned faces, brown leather cowboy boots and long chaps.

"You've made a great start," Star whispered in Laura's ear.

Laura grinned. But Star's words reminded her that no one knew who she was. How was she going to explain where she'd come from?

"We'll take this little fella to join the others," said the first cowboy. "Then we'll all rest up over there before we carry on." He nodded downriver, and Laura saw a huddle of wooden buildings not far away.

He held Star's reins while Laura climbed back into the saddle. "My name's Luke," he

said. "I don't think we've met before."

"Er . . . no," stammered Laura. "I . . . I live over there." She pointed towards the wooden houses and heard Star snort with approval.

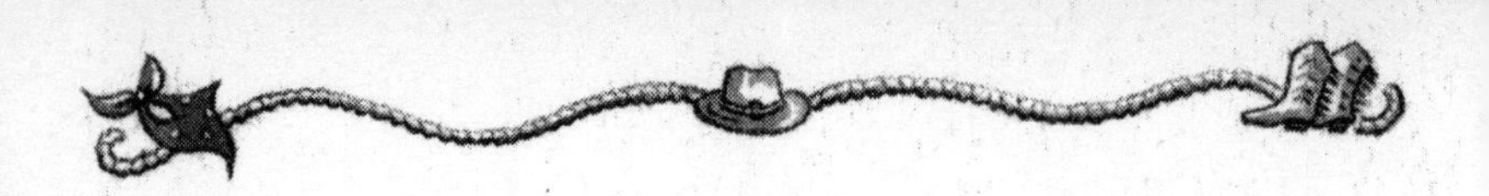

"Well, I'm the head cowboy," said Luke. "You've already met my daughter, Jolene." He nodded towards the girl in the yellow shirt.

"My name's Laura," said Laura. She smiled at Jolene, but, to her surprise, Jolene just scowled and turned her pony away.

With the calf trotting beside them, Laura and Star followed the other cowboys back to the slow-moving line of cattle. An older cowboy rode up on a pretty dun-coloured mustang.

"Well done," he said warmly. "You did really well to save that calf."

Laura jumped. He sounded just like Mr Barker from the fairground! She stared up at him curiously. He had wisps of white hair showing underneath his wide-brimmed felt

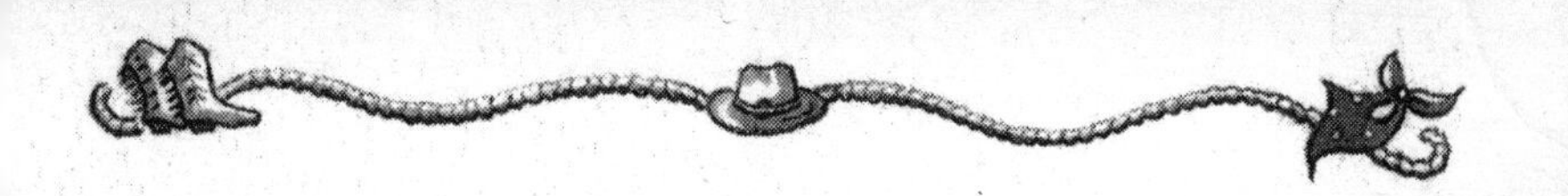

hat, and twinkling blue eyes. He *looked* just like Mr Barker too!

She was about to ask him what his name was when the cowboy touched the brim of his hat in farewell and rode ahead to join Luke and Jolene at the front of the drive.

Laura turned to another cowboy riding nearby. He was wearing a blue checked shirt and had a wisp of dry grass sticking out of his mouth. "Who was that?" she asked.

The cowboy stopped chewing the grass for a moment. "Oh, that's just old Red. He hasn't been on a cattle drive for ages, but he sure knows how to ride. I'm Hank, by the way." Just then, one of the cows began to stray out of line and he rode off to herd it back.

Laura watched him as he neck-reined his

pony to and fro, guiding the cow back to the others without upsetting it. Hank made it look so easy! Laura felt a thrill of delight. She was on a real-life cattle drive with her own magic pony!

"We'd better stay in the background here," Star said quietly as they drew closer to the wooden buildings.

"OK," whispered Laura. She leaned forward to stroke Star's neck. "Can anyone else hear you speak?" she asked.

Star shook her mane as though she was shaking off flies. "No," she replied. "To everyone else, it just sounds like neighs and whinnies. It's a special part of the carousel's magic – you picked the ticket with my name on and now we can understand each other!"

Laura grinned. What a fantastic secret!

"So what's the important thing that we have to do?" she said, remembering what the pony had said earlier. "Was it saving the calf?"

"I don't think so," said Star. "If it was, the Magic Carousel would have taken us back to the fairground by now. I expect it's a bigger task than that. We'll find out what it is together."

A bigger task! thought Laura. Wow! Laura loved detective movies nearly as much as Westerns, and now she could keep a sharp eye out for whoever it was that needed their help. But then she thought about her brothers, and suddenly felt worried. "But how long will it take?" she asked. "My brothers will wonder where I've gone."

Star twitched one ear. "You don't need to worry," she said reassuringly. "When you

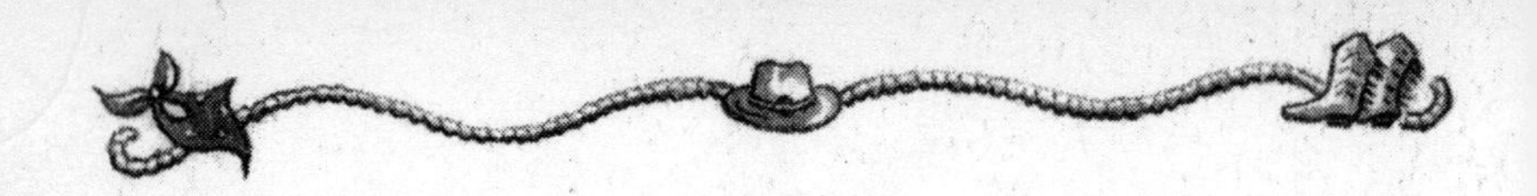

go back, no time will have passed at all!"

Laura felt thrilled. She wondered what her brothers would say if they could see her. It felt as if she was in a cowboy movie all of her own!

4. Jealous Jolene

They reached the little village of wooden houses and Laura tried to look as though she rode down the main street every day. But there was so much to look at! There were a few houses, a general store and a saloon bar – but not a single car! Laura could hardly imagine riding on a pony to get everywhere all the time. Near the bar, a young woman in a long dress was pumping water from a long-handled tap into a bucket. Laura watched the woman dip a tin mug into the bucket, then offer it to Hank as he rode past.

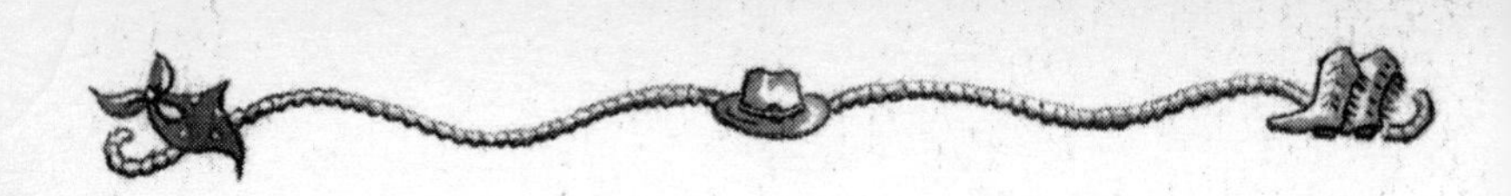

Hank thanked her and gulped down the water as if he was very thirsty. Laura saw Luke and Red ride up to the hitching rail by the saloon and dismount. She watched them carefully. Instead of taking both feet out of the stirrups at once, they swung themselves out of the saddle with their left foot still in place. Laura copied them, trying to look as casual as possible – but as she stepped down, she stumbled backwards and bumped into Jolene's pony.

"Careful!" snapped Jolene. "Smoky's jumpy enough today!"

"I'm sorry," said Laura.

Jolene looped Smoky's reins over the rail. "It was your fault that the calf jumped into the river," she told Laura over her shoulder.

Laura looked at Star in surprise. The calf had been startled when Smoky kicked the stone! Star gave a tiny shake of her head that only Laura could see. Laura knew she shouldn't quarrel with Jolene – the Magic Carousel hadn't brought her here to argue! She decided not to say anything about Smoky's mistake.

"You should have roped the calf as soon as it left the herd," Jolene added. She finished tying Smoky's reins and walked off towards the water pump.

Laura sighed. It looked like Jolene was

determined not to make friends. She stroked Star's soft muzzle, then reached up and rubbed the little white star on her forehead.

"Don't worry about Jolene," said Star. "She's probably just jealous because you rescued the calf and not her."

"What do you think I should do now?" Laura asked, feeling slightly nervous.

"You'll be fine," said Star. "Just keep an eye on the others."

All around her, the cowboys were climbing back on to their ponies.

"Let's go!" said Luke. "There's some wild country to get through before we reach the next camp."

Laura climbed into Star's saddle. "Shall we follow them?" she whispered. It was hard to know if they needed to go with the cow-

boys to find out their special task, or if they should stay behind in the little town.

Star scraped her front hoof on the ground as if she was thinking. "I think we should go with them," she said. "After all, I am a cow-girl's pony!"

Laura and Star cantered after the others. They soon caught up with the long line of cattle stretching into the distance. Up ahead, the rolling grassy plain ended in a line of rocky hills. Laura felt a flicker of excitement. That must be the wild country that Luke had mentioned.

But as Laura joined the back of the drive, Luke cantered over to her, frowning. "Hey, Laura!" he called. "You'll have to go back to the village now."

Laura's heart sank into her cowboy boots.

"We have a long way to go with these cows," Luke went on. "And I only take the most experienced cowboys and cowgirls on my cattle drives."

Laura thought quickly. She had to persuade Luke somehow! "My parents said I could join the next drive that passed through," she said. She gave Luke a pleading look. "*Please* let me come."

Just then, there was the sound of hoofs as another cowboy rode up. "What's going on here?" asked Red in a friendly voice.

Luke explained and Red smiled. "I think you should let her stay," he said. Laura's heart flipped over hopefully. "She saved the calf, remember?" Red reminded Luke. "She's obviously a good rider and she could be company for Jolene too."

There was a tiny moo from beside Star,

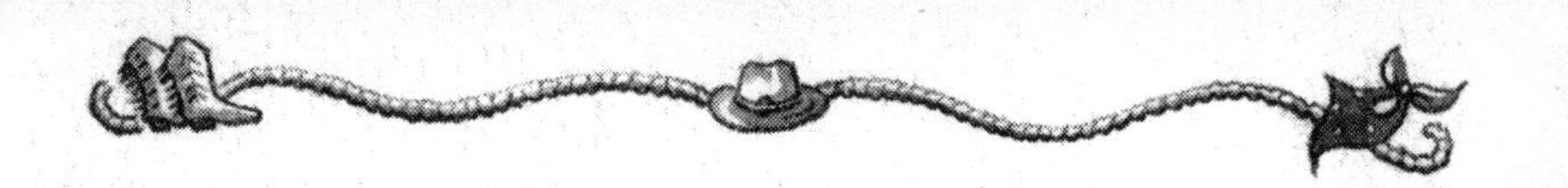

and Laura looked down to see the little calf trotting along close to Star's flank.

Red chuckled. "You see, Luke, you can't send her back. That calf has adopted Laura as his new mother. She'll have to look after him from now on."

Luke watched the calf for a moment, then smiled. "You're right, Red. I can't send her back now."

"Thanks, Luke," said Laura. "I won't let you down, I promise."

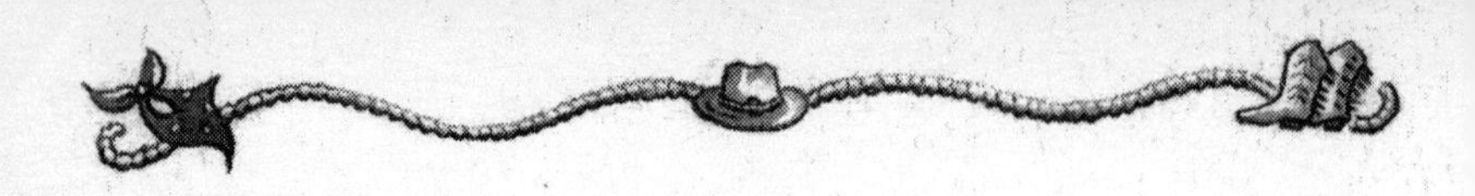

She looked down at the calf. He stared back with big adoring eyes, then mooed again. Laura smiled. He might not know it, but this time the calf had saved *her*! Now she had a special calf as well as a magic pony. She couldn't believe her luck!

As Red rode on ahead with Luke, the old cowboy turned and gave her a big wink.

On they rode, across the plains, with the rocky hills slowly drawing closer. The cowboys spread out along the line of cattle, keeping them from straying too far off the trail. It was hard work, because the cattle kept wandering off to graze on any tasty bit of grass they saw!

The land began to change – instead of swaying grass, Laura noticed prickly pear cactuses and boulders and bright yellow desert flowers. As they rode through a rocky

canyon, she saw a lizard slither between some stones and a hawk flying overhead, on the hunt for jackrabbits. And all the time the calf trotted along close to Star's feet. Laura smiled at her loyal new friend.

"I think we should give the calf a name," she said to Star. "What do you think we should call him?"

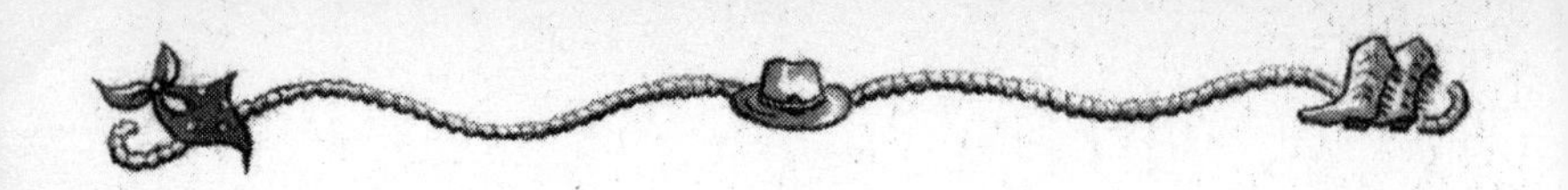

Star arched her neck and blew gently on the calf's ears. The calf twitched his ears happily. "Something to do with how you saved him?" she suggested.

"How *we* saved him," Laura corrected her, laughing. "How about Lucky?"

"Perfect!" agreed Star.

As daylight faded the men set about making a camp. The cattle were allowed to stop and graze, and Laura made sure that Lucky was settled among them. A young cow with a white patch on her nose sniffed at Lucky, then let the little calf graze next to her. Feeling relieved, Laura rode off to join the rest of the cowboys. As she dismounted, she couldn't believe how stiff she felt! She had never spent so long on a pony before, and

travelling across country was very different from trotting around a field at a riding school. But she wouldn't have missed a moment of the amazing adventure she'd had so far.

Star nuzzled her and Laura wrapped her arms around her pony's neck.

"Thank you, Star," she whispered. "This has been the best day of my life."

Star gave a happy whinny, then butted Laura with her nose. "You need to rest," she said. "It'll be another long day tomorrow."

But Laura was too excited to sit down. She watched as some of the others unbuckled bedrolls from the back of their saddles and laid them out on the ground. But Star didn't have a bedroll behind her saddle – what would Laura do? The ground looked very hard and uncomfortable. Then

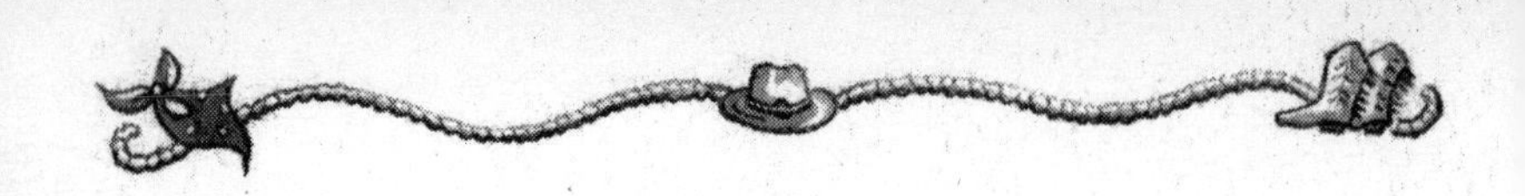

she saw Luke pass Jolene a bedroll and nod in Laura's direction. Jolene didn't look very happy, but she started to walk over to Laura.

"Here. You can borrow this one," Jolene said in a quiet voice, handing the bedroll over to Laura. It was a beautiful stripy red, yellow and blue blanket.

"Thank you!" Laura said, hoping that Jolene might be feeling more friendly. Jolene gave a thin smile and walked away. Laura watched her leave, then laid her blanket out near the horses, so that she could sleep close to Star. After making sure that Star had plenty of food and water, she set off to

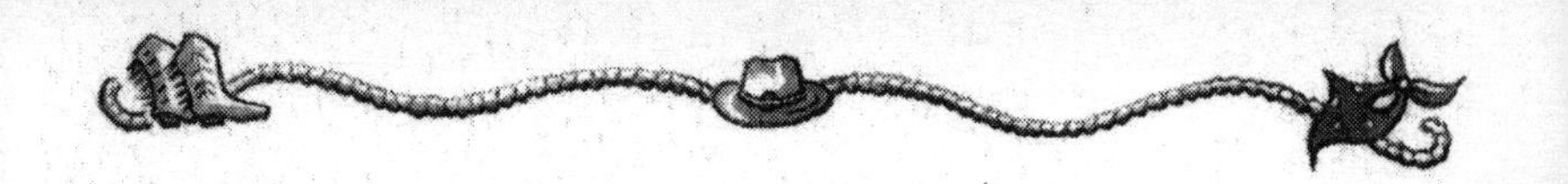

explore the camp. She had learned the names of all the cowboys during the long ride and already she felt as if she was part of the team.

Luke and Red were slowly riding around the cattle, keeping an eye on them, while Carlos the cook was unloading cooking equipment from the back of a pack mule. Tex and Mark were making a fire, with Jolene helping them. It was quickly getting cold now that the sun had set, and some of the cowboys wrapped themselves in colourful blankets when they sat down. Carlos began stirring a big pot of beef and bean stew on a smaller fire. It smelt delicious and Laura suddenly realized how hungry she was. She offered to help, and Carlos produced a stack of tin plates from one of his saddlebags.

"You can help me dish up," he said.

Laura gave Jolene a plate of stew first.

"Thanks," said Jolene without looking up.

"What about Luke and Red?" Laura asked Carlos when everyone had some food.

"Don't worry about them," Carlos told

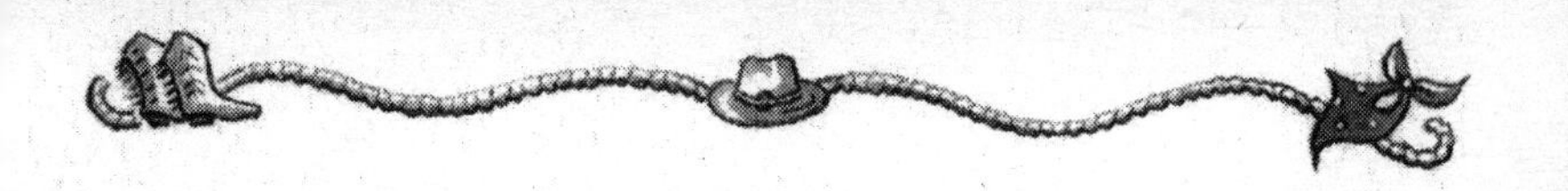

her. "I'll leave some stew in the pot and they'll eat when their shift's finished."

Laura felt a bit sorry for them – they must be really hungry! She sat down to eat her stew, thinking that being a cowboy was very hard work.

After a while, Laura noticed Jolene slip away to lie down in the shadows. Leaving the other cowboys sitting around the fire, Laura went over to her bedroll and found Lucky waiting for her sleepily! She snuggled into her warm stripy blanket.

"Good night, Star," she whispered.

"Sleep tight," her magic pony replied softly.

As Laura dozed off she heard the sound of singing. At first she thought it must be the men around the fire, but then she realized that it was coming from where the cattle

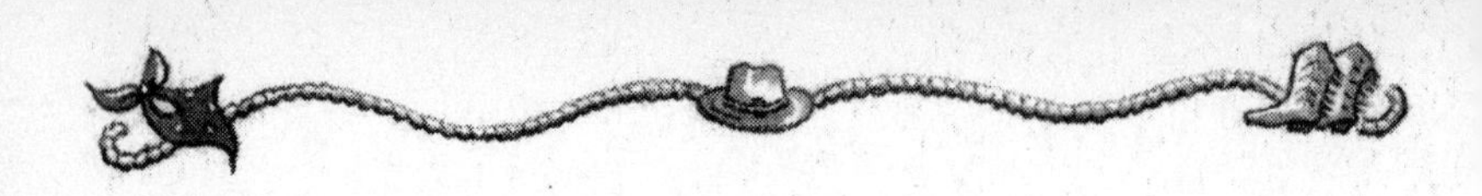

were grazing. It was Luke and Red, singing to them as they rode around! Laura smiled and began to drift deeper into sleep.

Suddenly a voice nearby jolted her awake.

". . . prices will be good enough," she heard.

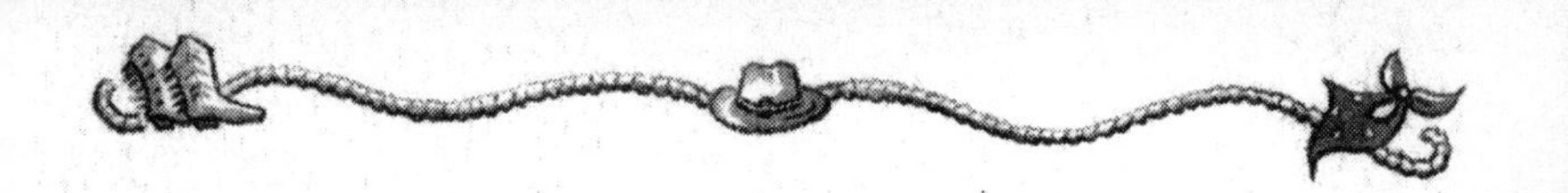

Laura opened her eyes. The singing had stopped. She had no idea how long she'd been asleep – perhaps Luke and Red had finished their shift by now.

". . . it will be easy money," said a muffled voice.

Laura felt her skin begin to prickle. There were definitely men talking nearby. And they weren't casually chatting – they were talking in urgent whispers, as though they were making a plan.

Laura lay as still as she could under her blanket, listening.

". . . just need to wait for half the cattle to go into the ravine," said one of the men.

"The secret valley near that ravine is going to be really useful!" said another. "We'd never be able to take the cattle without it."

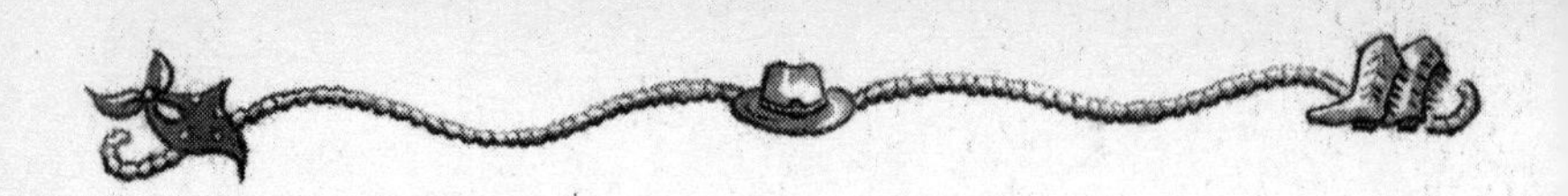

Laura's heart began to pound. Had she just overheard a plot to steal some of Luke's cattle?

5. Who Can Laura Trust?

Laura heard the men walk back towards the fire. They passed close to where she was lying and she held her breath. Suddenly one of them muttered crossly.

"What's wrong?" asked a companion.

"Nothing," replied the man. "Just a stupid cactus scratching my hand."

As the footsteps went past, crunching on the dry earth, Laura heard the rattling chink of a spur. She thought there were three men, but it could have been four. Her mind was racing. The men's voices had been

muffled by her blanket, which was tucked up around her ears, so she hadn't recognized any of the speakers. All she had were two tiny clues – one of the men had scratched his hand, and another was wearing a loose, jangling spur.

She heard the sound of one man mounting a horse, or maybe two. It was so annoying not to be sure! Laura wondered if Star was listening too, but she didn't dare call out to her. Soon the sound of singing started again, drifting on the night air. The rest of the camp grew quiet, and Laura peered out from underneath her blanket. She'd have to wait until morning to talk to Star. She stared up at the millions of stars stretching across the clear night sky. Only one thing was for sure: all three or four speakers had been men.

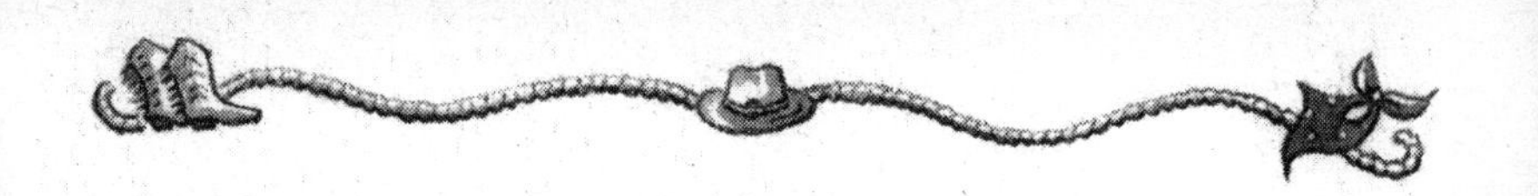

At last Laura drifted off to sleep again. When she woke, the grey-pink light of dawn streaked the sky. There was a chill in the air and she shivered. Sitting up, she pushed aside her blanket and tiptoed over to Star.

The cowgirl's pony was dozing, her eyes closed, but she woke up as Laura approached and whickered a friendly hello.

"Star!" whispered Laura, stroking her nose. "Last night I heard some of the men talking. I think they're planning to steal some of the cows. Did you hear anything?"

Star pricked up her ears. "No, not a thing. What happened?"

Quickly Laura told her everything. Star listened, her nostrils flaring.

"I think I know which ravine they're talking about," she said. "I overheard some of them talking about the route ahead

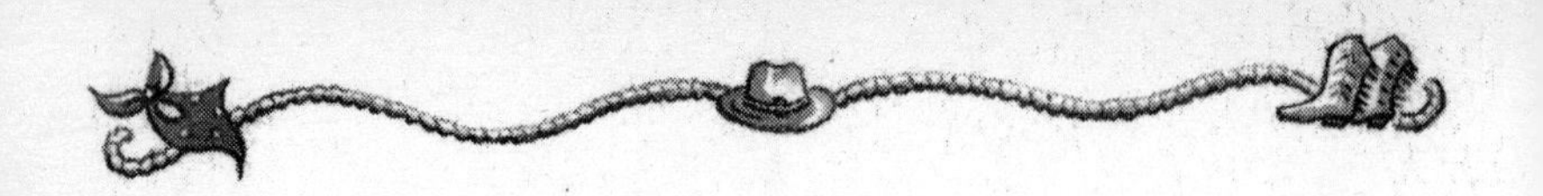

yesterday. There's one place where the trail gets really narrow."

"That must be it," agreed Laura. "What can we do? I don't know who was talking about the plot – though they were all men, so that rules out Jolene."

Star tossed her head. "Well, maybe you should ask her if she heard anything."

"But I don't think she likes me very much," Laura pointed out.

Star blew softly into Laura's blonde hair. "She was the only girl before you came along," Star reminded her. "Maybe she just needs some time to get used to you."

"We don't *have* time," said Laura. The camp was already beginning to stir – she could see Carlos lighting his fire to cook breakfast. "We'll get to the ravine today, and that's when the cowboys are planning to steal the cows!"

"Well," said Star, "we'll just have to hope that's enough time for you to make friends with Jolene."

When the cowboys had finished their breakfast, they packed up the camp and saddled their horses. Laura tried to strap her bedroll back into place behind Star's saddle. It was difficult, because the buckles were stiff.

"Do you need a hand there, Laura?" asked a kindly voice.

Laura looked around. Jesse was smiling down at her from his mustang. She yanked

on the stiffest buckle and the leather strap slipped into place.

"I'm fine, thanks." She smiled back at him.

"Well, you let me know if you need help with anything," he said.

He sounded so nice and friendly, and Laura hesitated. Surely he couldn't be one of the thieves? She needed to tell *someone*, and Jesse was just the sort of person she'd willingly trust! But just as she opened her mouth to speak, another of the cowboys, Mark, rode close by and gave Jesse a friendly slap on the shoulder. Laura snapped her mouth shut again. She knew the slap might not mean anything, but all the same it reminded her that *any* of the men could be thieves – even Jesse!

Laura swung herself into Star's saddle.

Lucky trotted over and greeted Laura with a friendly moo. Laura really wanted to check all the cowboys' spurs and whether any of them had a scratch on their hand, but it was impossible. The men quickly spread out around the herd, and with all the dust it was difficult to see anything clearly.

"You're right," Laura said to Star, patting the pony's neck. "I can't stop the thieves on my own. I'll have to speak to Jolene first."

6. Laura's Logic

The cattle began to move slowly onwards. Laura spotted Lucky in the middle of the herd and she felt glad that he seemed happy to be with the cattle again after his scary experience the day before. She could see Jolene's shiny black pigtails up ahead and realized that now was her chance to talk to her.

Laura nudged Star with her heels. "Let's catch up with Smoky and Jolene," she said.

"Good idea," Star said and broke into a canter. They soon caught up with the other

girl. But as they slowed down to a trot beside her, Jolene turned to them with her eyes blazing. "What d'you think you're doing?" she snapped. "You'll panic the cattle, cantering through them like that."

Laura was stung. She and Star hadn't cantered through the cattle, they'd cantered round them! *Why* didn't Jolene want to be her friend?

Out of the corner of her eye, Laura spotted a few cattle that were straying away from the others, and she pushed Star into another canter to guide them back to the rest of the herd. Once they were safely back in line, she trotted back to ride alongside Jolene again.

"Well done," Jolene said grudgingly. "Which ranch did you learn on?"

Laura wasn't sure what to say – she'd

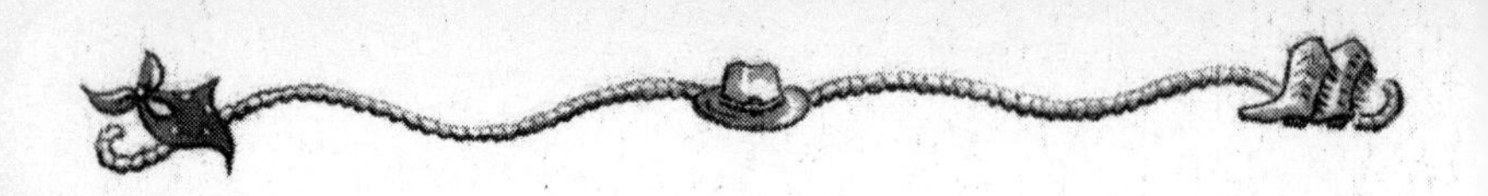

learned to ride at her local riding school, but she'd learned about Western riding from movies! She couldn't say *that.* She thought quickly. "Oh, a place called Shady Creek," she said casually. Well, it was *almost* true. It was the ranch in her favourite Western storybook.

"Never heard of it," said Jolene. She shrugged. "I guess it must be pretty good."

Laura grinned. She was glad to hear the other girl say something nice at last! She patted Star's neck. "Well, I wouldn't be much good without Star," she said, and for the first time, Jolene gave her a friendly smile.

It was too good an opportunity to miss. Laura took a deep breath. "I think some of the cowboys are planning to steal half the cattle," she said. "I heard them talking about

it last night. They're going to use a secret valley near a ravine."

Jolene stared at her as if she was crazy, and then laughed. "There's no secret valley round here. You must have been dreaming."

Laura's heart sank. Maybe she'd got it wrong. After all, Jolene knew the trail much better than she did.

But then Star tossed her head and gave a

whinny. "If Jolene knew about the valley, it wouldn't be secret," she pointed out.

It was true. Laura knew she had to keep trying. "I'm sure I heard right," she insisted.

Jolene rolled her eyes. "My dad knows all these guys really well. He would never use thieves on his cattle drive," she said. She raised one eyebrow. "Maybe you think my dad's a thief too?"

"No!" Laura protested. "I just know what I heard, that's all. There were three or four men speaking and one of them had a loose spur. Another scratched his hand on a cactus."

Jolene shook her head disbelievingly. A big cow wandered out of line up ahead, and she kicked Smoky with her heels.

"Now what?" exclaimed Laura, watching Jolene canter away to round up the cow.

"You did your best," said Star. "We'll just have to think of something else."

"Some*thing* else!" Laura echoed in despair. "Some*one* else is what we need. I can't help at all. The carousel must have made a mistake!"

"No, no, that doesn't happen," Star said, shaking her mane. "The Magic Carousel always chooses the right person to help!"

But right now Laura didn't feel so sure . . .

The sun rose in the sky, and the air grew hotter and hotter. The trail began to narrow, with craggy rocks towering up on either side in deep yellows and reds, contrasting with the lovely blue sky.

"The ravine must be getting close now,"

Laura said to Star, who nodded her head in agreement. Laura felt butterflies fluttering in her stomach. Then she noticed that one of the cowboys had dropped back and was dismounting his horse.

Laura raised a hand to shield her eyes from the sun, and saw that it was Hank. She turned to Tex, the cowboy nearest to her. "Is Hank OK?" she called.

"Oh sure," replied Tex. "He's just fixing his spur. It got loose yesterday."

Laura gulped. Hank must be the thief with the clinking spur! "Star, what can I *do*?" she muttered.

"Stay calm," said Star. "The ravine's just up ahead."

Laura looked desperately around for Luke, but he was right at the front of the herd, at the entrance to a narrow gap

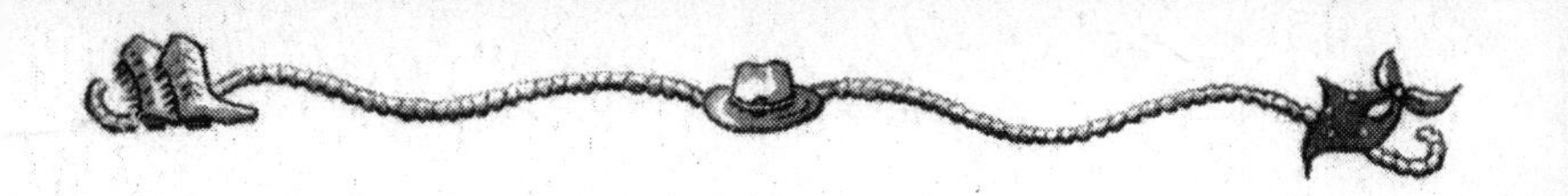

between the rocks. She saw him cup his hands around his mouth.

"We're taking the first cattle in!" Luke called. "Follow on behind, not too fast!"

He turned his horse and rode alongside the first cows into the ravine. Laura stared after him. Should she gallop up to Luke and tell him what she'd heard? While she was trying to decide, Tex wheeled his horse around in front of her – and as he did, Laura noticed his hand. It had a deep scratch on it!

Tex cantered off in a cloud of dust towards Hank, who was still at the back of the herd. A piece of paper fluttered out of Tex's saddlebag as he cantered away, and got caught up in the branches of a thorn-bush. But Laura was too busy wondering

what to do next to look closely at it. Everything was happening so quickly!

"Tex must be one of the thieves too!" she whispered to Star. "Come on, Star. Let's go and talk to Jolene again. She's the only person we can trust!"

7. Stop, Thieves!

Jolene frowned as Laura cantered up to her. "What have you heard now?" she asked. "Is my dad about to run off with everyone's horses?"

"No, Jolene, please listen," Laura begged her breathlessly. "Hank and Tex have gone right to the back of the drive. Hank has a loose spur and Tex has a scratch on his hand. They must be the cowboys I heard talking last night!"

Jolene still looked doubtful. For one awful moment, Laura thought she was about to

ride away. "You've got to believe me!" she insisted. "I couldn't have dreamed all that. You must help me, before it's too late!" But Jolene didn't seem to be listening. She pointed at a thorn-bush just behind Laura.

"What's that?" Jolene asked. "I saw it fall out of Tex's bag!"

So Jolene had noticed too! Star trotted over to the thorn-bush. Laura leaned down and peered at the thick black writing on the piece of paper. "*Cattle sale!*" she exclaimed. She

snatched the paper from the bush, then trotted back to Jolene.

"Look at this," Laura said, handing Jolene the paper. "There's a big cattle sale taking place tomorrow. The thieves must be planning on selling the cattle there."

Jolene's eyes opened wide as she read about the sale. "It's in a town on the other side of the hills," she muttered. She looked up in amazement. "You must be right. But I've never heard of a secret valley."

Laura felt a rush of relief that Jolene believed her at last. "We have to stop the thieves!" she declared. "Let's go and warn your dad!"

Jolene looked down the line of cattle that were walking steadily forwards, and Laura followed her gaze. There was no sign of

Red, Carlos or Juan – they had all followed Luke into the ravine.

"We can't," Jolene whispered.

Laura frowned. "What do you mean?"

Jolene looked very worried. "We can't warn my dad or Red or any of the others. They've already gone into the ravine."

Laura was puzzled. "Can't we catch them up? We could ride along the top of the ravine and canter down ahead of the cattle."

Jolene shook her head. "The sides are too steep and rocky. You can't canter down them and even if we could, we might scare the cattle."

Laura gulped. She looked around. There were only four cowboys left at the back of the herd – Hank and Tex, and Jesse and Mark, whom Laura had thought were so

nice! As Laura watched, Hank and Tex left the others and cantered to the ravine entrance. They walked their horses into the mouth of the narrow gap, stopping the rest of the cattle from walking through.

Jolene's blue eyes flashed in anger. "They're dividing the herd in half!" she exclaimed.

It was true. As the cattle milled about in confusion at the entrance to the ravine, Jesse and Mark began to guide them away from the main trail, towards the hills.

Laura wheeled Star around. "Come on, Jolene! We'll stop them ourselves!"

8. The Heat Is On!

Side by side, Laura and Jolene galloped up to Hank.

"Hank, what d'you think you're doing?" Jolene shouted. "You can't steal the cattle. You'll never get away with it!"

Hank looked surprised just for an instant. Then he threw back his head and laughed. "Too late!" he hollered. "There's nothing you can do to stop us now!"

Laura heard Tex laugh as well and she felt a surge of anger. But she and Jolene couldn't turn the cattle around by themselves,

not with four cowboys to stop them!

As the last of the cows plodded after their stolen companions, Hank and Tex cantered off behind them, waving their hats in a mocking salute.

"So long, Jolene!" called Tex.

Jolene's cheeks flushed scarlet in fury. "We'll follow them!" she declared. "We must be able to stop them somehow!"

She urged Smoky forward, and he jumped straight into a gallop.

Star shook her mane. "I think we need to come up with a plan," she said.

Laura agreed. She stared at the rocky hills ahead of

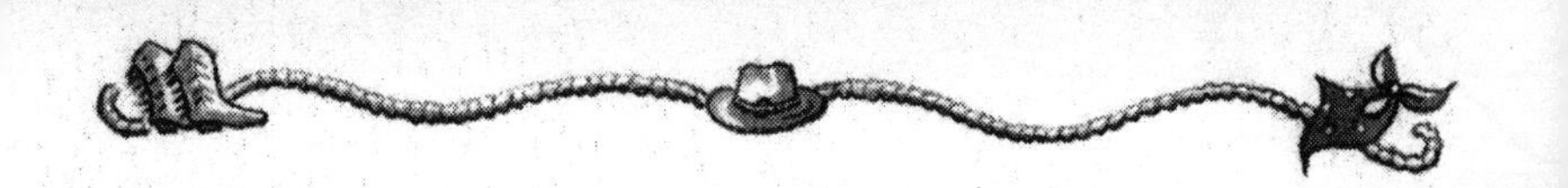

them. The cattle were disappearing one by one between a gap in the rocks. That must be the entrance to the secret valley!

"Wait!" she shouted after Jolene. "Come back!"

Looking annoyed, Jolene cantered back. "Come *on*!" she said. "We can't let them get away!"

"I know," said Laura. "But we have to try to get in front of the herd. Once they are in the secret valley it won't be easy to get past the cattle without the four cowboys seeing us." She pointed at the hill beside the narrow gap. "But if we could climb up there, we might be able to overtake them."

Jolene stared at the hillside. "That slope's pretty steep," she said doubtfully.

"I can manage it," whinnied Star.

Laura gratefully stroked the mare's neck.

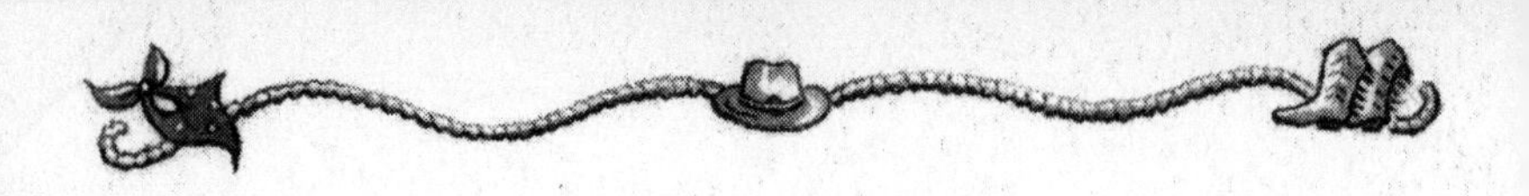

Star was so brave and loyal! "I think we should try," she said to Jolene. "Once we're ahead of the cattle, we'll be able to ride straight at them. They'll turn around in panic and we'll be able to drive them back down the valley."

Jolene thought for a moment. "It might work," she said at last. "Let's go!"

The two ponies began to pick their way up the side of the hill, puffing and blowing as they struggled up the rocky slope. When they reached the top, a cooling breeze blew against the girls' cheeks. Laura steered Star carefully along the ridge and looked down into the secret valley. It made her feel very dizzy! There was the line of cows, plodding along with the cowboys riding

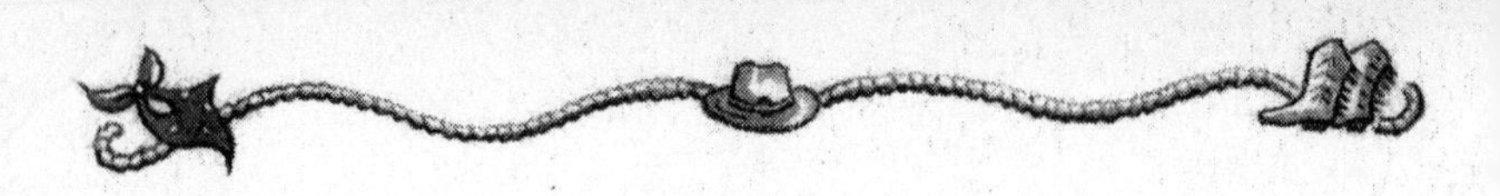

beside them. Laura took a deep breath. It was so beautiful here – exactly how she'd always imagined it from her favourite movies. But she wasn't here to enjoy the view. They had to stop the cattle thieves!

The ponies trotted along the ridge until they had overtaken the cattle far below. Laura's stomach turned somersaults all the way – she desperately hoped the cowboys wouldn't look up! Fortunately, the cowboys were too busy guiding the cows to spare a glance at the ridge above them.

Once they were well ahead of the herd, Laura began to look for a good place for their ambush. They needed a gentle slope, so that Smoky and Star wouldn't stumble as they galloped down. At last they found the perfect spot, just around a bend in the valley. All they had to do now was stand still . . . and wait.

The girls listened, waiting for the sound of cattle hoofs. The valley was silent apart from the shrill cry of a hawk. Laura gripped her reins more firmly. We can do it, she told herself.

Suddenly Jolene pointed down the valley, where dust was beginning to rise in a pale yellow cloud. "They're coming!"

The first cow appeared along the track, with two more close behind . . . then two more . . . and there was Hank, riding alongside them.

Laura patted Star's neck. "Any minute now," she whispered.

Jolene stared down at the herd of cattle. "I still can't believe they're doing this to my dad," she muttered. "If he loses half the herd,

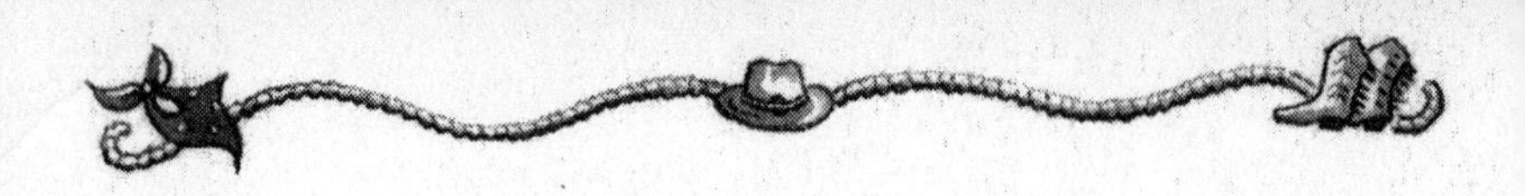

no one will ever use him as a trail boss again. They're meant to be his friends!"

"I know," agreed Laura, watching the line of cows get longer and longer. "But we're going to stop them, I promise."

Jolene nodded, her eyes sparking with determination. There was a pause, then –

"NOW!" both girls shouted at once.

With a snort, Star plunged down the slope towards the cattle. Smoky followed, and the girls waved and hollered at the top of their voices.

"Wooo-wooo-wooo!" yelled Laura, waving her lasso above her head. "Go on, Star!"

Star galloped towards the first cows, her mane blowing in the wind and her nostrils flaring. The cows stared at her in alarm – then started bellowing in fear. In seconds, the whole herd was leaping and scrambling

around, fighting to gallop back the way they'd come. Laura caught sight of Hank and Tex. Their horses had panicked when the cows started stampeding, and they were both rearing up with their front hoofs

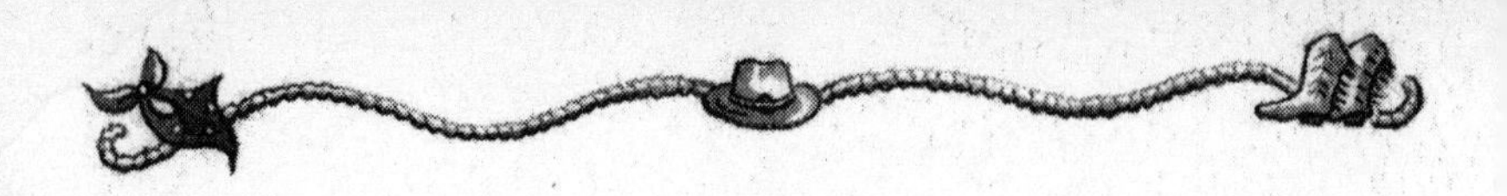

pawing the air. Laura just had time to glimpse both the cowboys struggling to stay on – and then all she could see was dust, with cattle thundering past, out of the secret valley and back the way they'd come.

"We have to get to the front!" yelled Jolene. "We have to slow them down before they reach the ravine!"

There was only one way to get to the ravine ahead of the frightened cows, and that was to gallop straight through the middle of them. The cows were stampeding already, so for once it didn't make any difference that Laura wasn't riding carefully around the edge of the herd. She clung on as Star surged forward, leaping over boulders and bushes. Laura didn't have to tell her what to do at all – the clever cowgirl's pony already knew! Out of

the corner of her eye, Laura could see Jolene and Smoky galloping through the cattle as well. Jolene was slightly ahead of Laura.

After a few breathless minutes, Laura and Star arrived back at the main track and joined Jolene. She was calming the cattle down as they emerged from the secret valley by cantering in front of them and calling to them in a soothing voice. Laura copied her, and at last they managed to bring the cattle at the front of the herd back down to a trot.

"Try to let them into the ravine a few at a time," called Jolene. "That way they won't hurt themselves."

Laura and Star blocked part of the way so that the cattle trotted past them one at a time, or just two by two. They eyed Star

nervously, but she now stood still and calm with her ears pricked up.

Laura let out a long sigh of relief. "We did it!" she called to Jolene.

"We sure did!" Jolene agreed.

They followed the last of the cows into the ravine. Laura looked back to see if the thieves had come out of the secret valley yet, but there was no sign of them. Suddenly Luke galloped around a corner up ahead. Laura guessed he had realized half the herd was missing.

"Dad! We rescued them!" called Jolene, waving at him over the backs of the cows. Luke listened in amazement as Jolene told him everything that had happened. "It was all Laura's idea!" she finished.

Laura smiled happily. "This was our task, wasn't it?" she whispered to Star.

The pony tossed her mane so that it

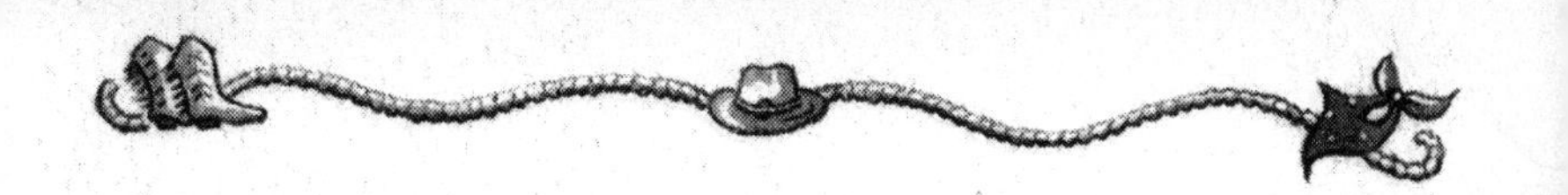

flicked lightly against Laura's fingers. "Yes, and we did brilliantly!" she whinnied.

There was the sound of hoofs behind them, and Laura twisted around in her saddle to see the four thieves cantering into the ravine. They pulled their horses to a halt when they spotted Luke. Laura held her breath, waiting to see what would happen next.

Luke started to gallop over to the thieves. "Hey, you!" he said. But before he reached them, the four cowboys turned and raced away in a cloud of dust.

Luke slowed his pony and trotted back to the girls. "They won't get away with this," he promised grimly. "When we reach the next town, I'll make sure everyone knows what they tried to do. They'll be in big trouble when the sheriff catches up with them!"

Laura exchanged a delighted grin with

Jolene. With the help of their brilliant ponies, they'd saved the herd!

Later that night, around a roaring campfire, Laura sat next to Jolene, wrapped in her stripy blanket. The camp felt small now that there were only four cowboys left, but Luke said he would be able to find more drivers when they reached the town.

Carlos cooked an extra-special meal to celebrate, and Juan played lively tunes on his violin for the girls to clap along to. Lucky the calf left the herd for a while and came to stand beside Laura and Jolene as they sat together on a log. Laura felt a bit worried. She and Star had saved the cows, but what would happen to Lucky when the Magic Carousel took her home?

Just then, Lucky nuzzled his nose into the back of Jolene's neck. Jolene laughed and reached up to stroke his furry brown ears. And suddenly Laura knew Lucky would be just fine without her, because Jolene would always look after him.

Next morning, Laura only woke up when Red shook her gently by the shoulder. It was

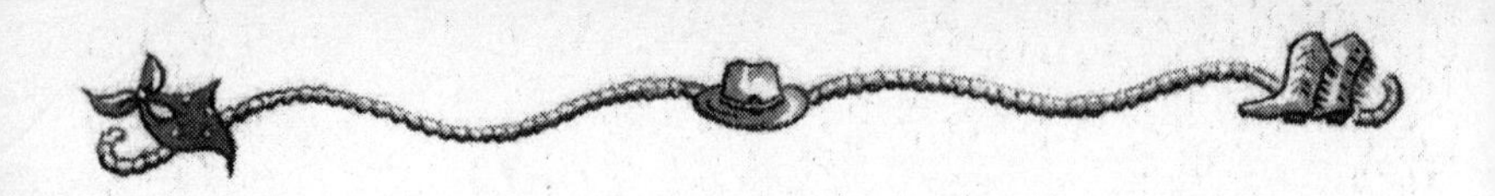

another beautiful day. Sleepily, Laura packed away her bedroll and took it over to Star.

"Hello, Star," she whispered, stroking her warm chestnut neck. She knew that today would be her last day on the cattle drive, now that they had finished their task.

As they rode, the trail began to widen, and the cowboys passed other riders and a few rickety chuck wagons, throwing up clouds of dust from their wooden wheels. Laura patted Star's neck and peered through the dust at Red, who was riding a little way ahead. The sunlight glinted on a metal buckle on his hat, and Laura felt as if she was in a golden haze of sparkling light.

Snatches of music began to play, and Laura looked around, puzzled. Where was it coming from? Then she realized that the hot dusty plain had faded away and she was

surrounded by twinkling lights, flashing in pretty colours. The Magic Carousel came smoothly to a halt and Laura looked down. Star's neck was no longer soft and warm. Her body and mane were made of painted wood once more. But her chestnut ears were still pricked up and, as she slid out of the saddle, Laura was sure she heard her give one last little whinny.

Laura reached up and touched the pony's little white star. "Thanks so much," she whispered.

Her fringe fell across her face and, as she pushed it back behind her ear, Laura felt something stuck in her hair. She pulled it out and looked down at it in surprise. It was a stem of prairie grass! Laura closed her fingers around it, picturing the endless grassy plains. Riding on the cattle drive had been the greatest adventure of her life, and now she had something to remember Star by forever!

Jump on board the Magic Pony Carousel for a whole lot of fun! You can find out more about the Magic Ponies plus play fun pony games and download cool activities.

Log on now at

www.magicponycarousel.com

Poppy Shire

The sparkly mist cleared away, leaving Sophie and Jewel standing alone in the darkness at a crossroads on a grassy heath. Sophie looked around, feeling utterly bewildered. A minute ago she'd been at a noisy, colourful fairground – and now she was in the middle of nowhere, in the middle of the night! She patted Jewel's wooden neck for comfort.

To her amazement, he snorted and shook his head. Jewel wasn't wooden at all! He was a real pony. Sophie stroked his thick, warm mane, and he reached his head round to nuzzle at her hand.

"What's going on?" Sophie breathed. "Where are we?"

Books coming in 2006

The prices shown below are correct at the time of going to press. However, Macmillan Publishers reserves the right to show new retail prices on covers, which may differ from those previously advertised.

Title	ISBN	Price
Magic Pony Carousel: Sparkle	0 330 44041 1	£3.99
Magic Pony Carousel: Brightheart	0 330 44042 X	£3.99
Magic Pony Carousel: Star	0 330 44043 8	£3.99
Magic Pony Carousel: Jewel	0 330 44044 6	£3.99
Magic Pony Carousel: Crystal	0 330 44597 9	£3.99
Magic Pony Carousel: Flame	0 330 44598 7	£3.99